Postman Pat

Sara Clifton

SIMON AND SCHUSTER

Sara Clifton
Forge Cottage
Garner Bridge
Greendale

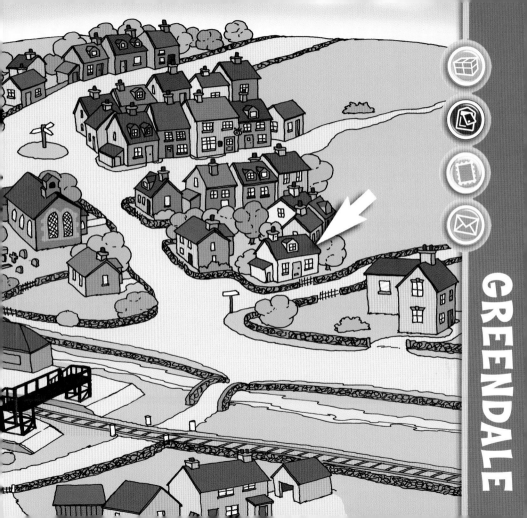

GREENDALE

Come and say hello to Sara Clifton!

Everyone loves Postman Pat's wife — and not just for her prize-winning cakes! Sara is always cheerful, whether she's running the café with her friend, Nisha, or helping out at Greendale Primary. What would Julian and Pat do without her?

Julian had been helping Pat on the Saturday delivery round.

"That's good timing," smiled Sara, when they got in. "I'm just dishing up lunch."

"Yippee, I'm starving!" cheered Julian.

"There's a letter for you here," smiled Pat, taking his seat at the table.

Sara opened it up. "It's from Aunt Gladys! Goodness, I haven't seen her in ages."

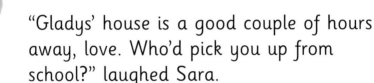

Sara read the letter from cover to cover, then read it again.

"Why don't you go and see her, Mum?" asked Julian.

"Gladys' house is a good couple of hours away, love. Who'd pick you up from school?" laughed Sara.

"What about me?" asked Pat. "Work is quiet at the moment. I could even do your shift at the café."

Sara wasn't too sure. "I don't know about that..."

But Pat wouldn't take no for an answer. After a quick ring to Aunt Gladys, Sara's trip was booked.

"There'll be a fair bit to do," worried Sara. "I'll call Nisha and ask her to help."

Julian giggled. "It's only one day, Mum, Dad can cope!"

"Just leave me a list and I'll make sure everything's sorted," grinned Pat.

"Now, I've cooked a casserole. Just pop it in the oven at three," said Sara, as she got on the train a few days later.

"You just have a good time," smiled Pat.

"I'm so excited!" Sara grinned. "Bye!"

Pat waved then pulled out the list his wife had written. "Right, back home to make scones for the café."

It took Pat all morning to get to grips with the scones.

"Now is this plain or self-raising flour?" he mumbled.

"Miaow!" Poor Jess was covered in white powder. Before Pat could apologise, the phone rang.

"Oh hello, Nisha," answered Pat. "Is it twelve already? I'll be right there."

Pat pulled a rather flat batch of scones out of the oven. "Come on, Jess, we're late!"

The café was already getting busy when Pat arrived. "Tuna mayo for me," shouted Sylvia Gilbertson, "on brown, please!"

"Hello, Pat!" smiled Nisha. "Can you pop on an apron and start taking orders?"

"Bacon for me too, but with ketchup on white," added Ted Glen.

Pat started scribbling in his pad, but by the time he made it to the kitchen he was feeling a bit overwhelmed.

"Thank heavens for that!" sighed Pat, when lunchtime was over.

"There were a few mix-ups, but we made it in the end," said Nisha.

"Sorry about the scones," Pat added, before sitting down. "I think I need a little rest after that rush!"

"No time for that," said Nisha. "You have to get Julian from football practise."

Pat arrived at the school playground just as Jeff Pringle blew his whistle.

"Well done, team! Very good passing today."

The Greendale kids cheered, then took off their football shirts. Julian started to stuff them into a big holdall.

"What's all this, son?" asked Pat.

"Mum always washes the team kit," explained Julian.

"How does she manage it?" wondered Pat, lifting the bag over his shoulder.

"I'm home!" called Sara, an hour later.

"Just in time for tea," said Julian, leaping up to say hello.

"Tea?" said Pat. "Oh no — I forgot to cook the casserole!"

Sara grinned, then placed hot fish and chips on the table. "I thought you might have your hands full."

"Sara Clifton," smiled Pat, giving his wife a hug, "you think of everything!"

SIMON AND SCHUSTER

First published in 2006 in Great Britain by Simon & Schuster UK Ltd.
Africa House, 64-78 Kingsway, London WC2B 6AH
A CBS COMPANY

Text by Mandy Archer © 2006 Simon & Schuster UK Ltd
Illustrations by Baz Rowell © 2006 Simon & Schuster UK Ltd

ISBN 1416916474
EAN 9781416916475
Printed in China
1 3 5 7 9 10 8 6 4 2